Published by Top That! Publishing plc
Tide Mill Way, Woodbridge, Suffolk, IP12 1AP, UK
www.topthatpublishing.com
Illustrations copyright © 2013 Top That! Publishing plc
Text copyright © 2013 Joanna Gray
All rights reserved
0 2 4 6 8 9 7 5 3 1
Printed and bound in China

Creative Director – Simon Couchman
Editorial Director – Daniel Graham

Written by Joanna Gray
Illustrated by Dubravka Kolanovic

ISBN 978-1-78244-040-6

A catalogue record for this book is available from the British Library
Printed and bound in China

The Little Raindrop
by Joanna Gray

'For Nathan, Will and Karin. Thank you for inspiring me.'
Joanna Gray

One dark and stormy day, a little raindrop fell out of a cloud and flew faster and faster through the sky.

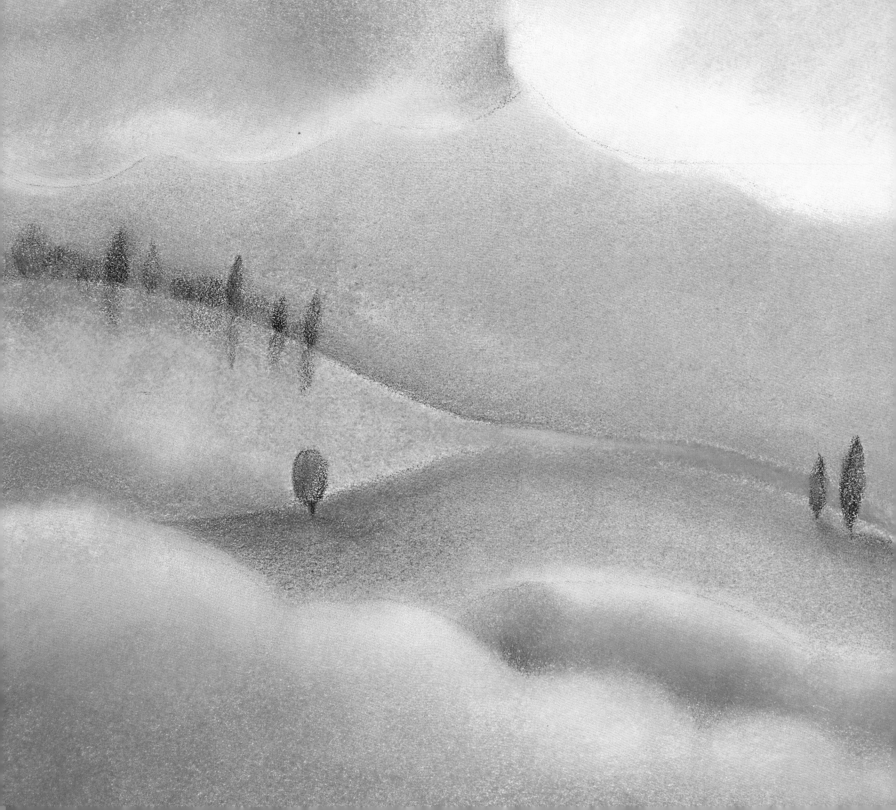

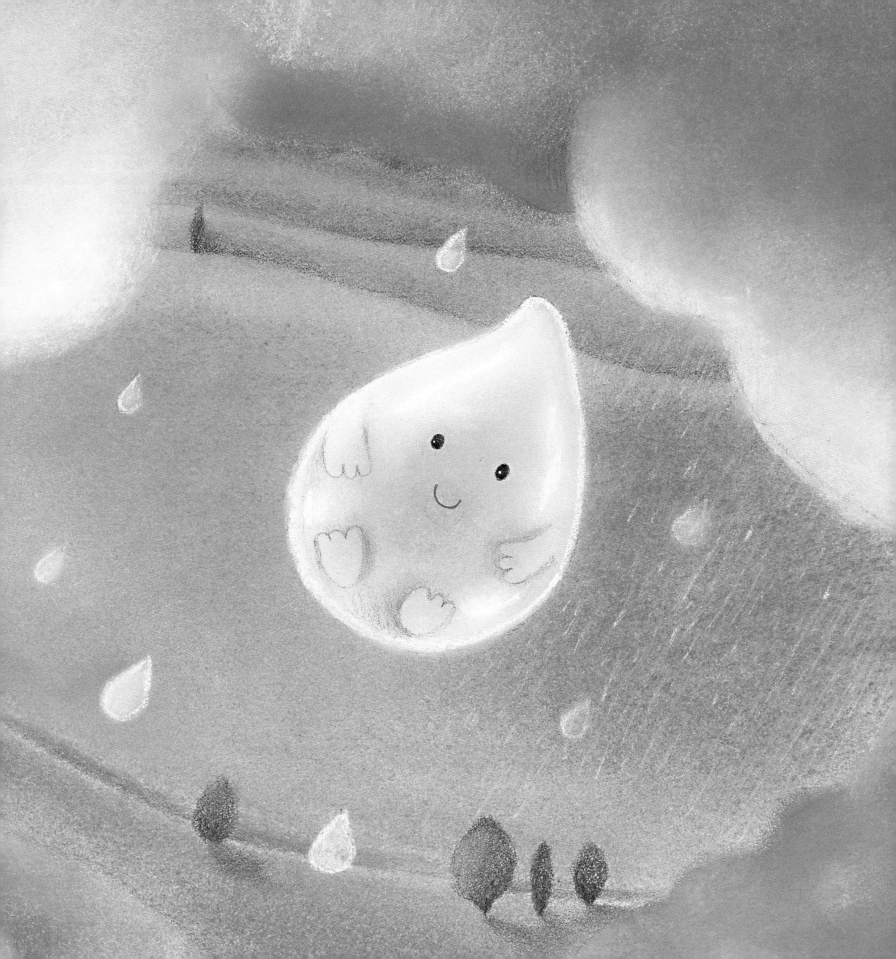

A gust of wind blew Little Raindrop sideways and in a dazzling flash of red, orange and yellow, he found himself inside a rainbow.

Enjoying the beautiful colours, Little Raindrop
fell through green, blue, indigo and violet before
another gust of wind blew him out of the rainbow.

Splash! Little Raindrop landed in a shallow
puddle on top of a large rock.

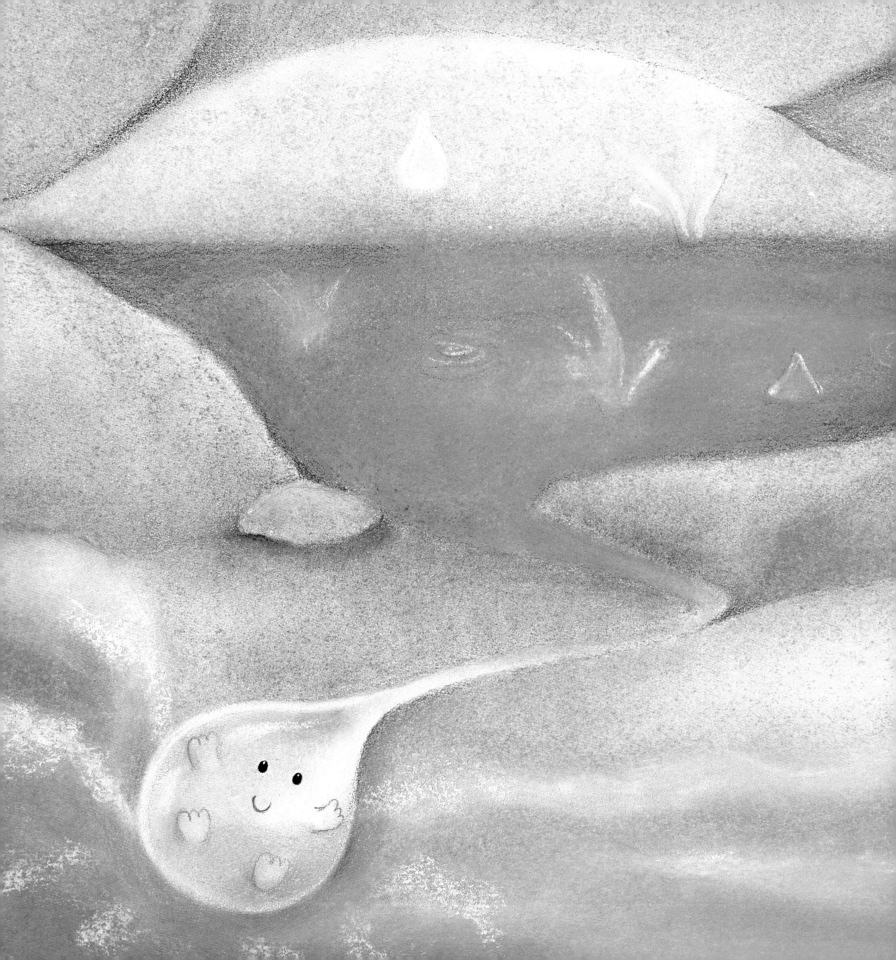

Splish! Splash! Splosh!
Lots of other raindrops fell all
around him, until the puddle
was overflowing.

Little Raindrop ran down
the side of the rock and
joined a stream.

In the stream, Little Raindrop
drifted through woods and bounced
over pebbles.

He played with small, shimmering fish
and watched them dart around
as deer and rabbits came to drink
at the water's edge.

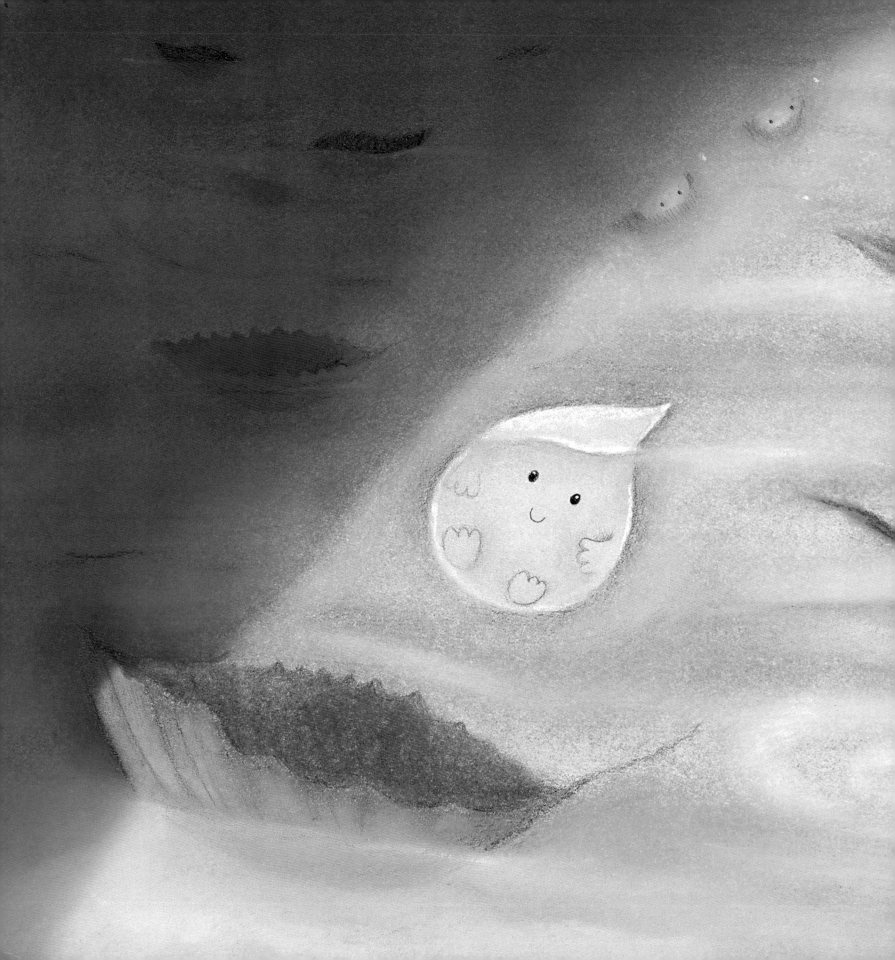

Sometimes, laughing children would race sticks in the water and Little Raindrop would chase them under bridges, dodging the swirling grass and fluttering leaves.

After a while, the stream joined a river and Little Raindrop floated along in the strong current.

At times, the river was calm and peaceful and Little Raindrop watched diving kingfishers and larger fish, as they swam slowly by.

At other times, the river
was noisy and rough.
Little Raindrop raced
along rapids and dived
down waterfalls, carefully
avoiding the jagged rocks
at the bottom of the falls.

Eventually, the river reached the sea and Little Raindrop was pulled far away from the shore.

He met friendly dolphins, who played and danced in the sunlight, and listened as they whistled and clicked their greetings to each other.

One day, the tide pulled Little Raindrop back to the beach. He surfed the waves and crashed onto the shore until finally he came to rest on the soft sand.

The sun shone down on the sand and Little
Raindrop got hotter and hotter, until the
warmth of the sun drew him up into the air.

It was cooler in the sky and Little Raindrop
joined a cloud that was already
full of other raindrops.

Little Raindrop was ready to fall to Earth
and begin his journey once more.

More great picture books from Top That! Publishing

ISBN 978-1-84956-610-0

A fox cub experiences his first summer in this heart-warming storybook.

ISBN 978-1-78244-064-2

A humorous storybook, full of nonsense, by inimitable author, Edward Lear.

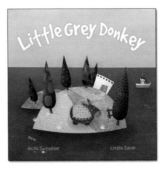

ISBN 978-1-84956-245-4

Unique illustrations capture the loving bond between two best friends!

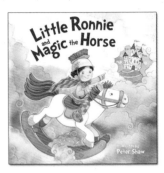

ISBN 978-1-84956-778-7

A fantastical tale about a boy and the adventures he has with his rocking horse.

ISBN 978-1-78244-074-1

Cammy the colourful Chameleon learns an important lesson in this vibrant tale.

ISBN 978-1-84956-304-8

Milly the meerkat learns a very important lesson in this classic tale.

ISBN 978-1-84956-302-4

Follow the antics of the escaped zoo animals as they cause pandamonium!

ISBN 978-1-78244-059-8

Peter's pebbles come to life in this perfectly crafted tale, full of imagination.

ISBN 978-1-78244-073-4

This tale, full of fun and folly, recalls the Quangle Wangle and his delightful hat.

ISBN 978-1-84956-424-3

A wise owl refuses to bow to peer pressure in this amusing, rhyming tale.

ISBN 978-1-84956-438-0

A fantastical tale about unruly, morning hair and a mischievous fairy.

ISBN 978-1-84956-439-7

The animal food chain is turned upside-down in this funny story with a twist.

Available from all good bookstores or visit www.topthatpublishing.com